SPORTS SUPERSTARS

KEVIN DURANT

By Anthony K. Hewson

WORLD BOOK

Your Front Row Seat to the Games

This edition is co-published by agreement between
Kaleidoscope and World Book, Inc.

Kaleidoscope Publishing, Inc.
6012 Blue Circle Drive
Minnetonka, MN 55343 U.S.A.

World Book, Inc.
180 North LaSalle St., Suite 900
Chicago IL 60601 U.S.A.

Kaleidoscope ISBNs
978-1-64519-039-4 (library bound)
978-1-64494-197-3 (paperback)
978-1-64519-140-7 (ebook)

World Book ISBN
978-0-7166-4342-5 (library bound)

Library of Congress Control Number
2019940059

Printed in the United States of America.

TABLE OF
CONTENTS

CHAPTER 1

Becoming Golden

With the championship on the line, Kevin Durant was calm. The ball bounced off the hoop. Durant jumped. Using his long arms, he grabbed the **rebound**. Then he turned up court.

Less than a minute remained in Game 3 of the 2017 National Basketball Association (NBA) Finals. Durant's Golden State Warriors were down by two points. Superstar LeBron James and his Cleveland Cavaliers sensed the win. But Durant showed no fear.

San Francisco City Hall lit up in Golden State Warriors colors

Kevin Durant was a key player for the Golden State Warriors in the 2017 NBA Finals.

Durant rises above LeBron James for a three-pointer in Game 3 of the 2017 NBA Finals.

Durant calmly dribbled up the court. In an instant, he pulled up. James tried to step in. It was too late. The 6-foot-9 (2.1 m) Durant jumped straight up. He rose high above James's outstretched arm. Then, Durant flicked his wrist. **Swish**. The ball dropped through the hoop. It was a three-pointer. That put the Warriors up 114–113.

Durant admired his shot for a moment. But 45 seconds remained. So he quickly shuffled back on defense.

Cleveland needed a basket. The Warriors guarded the Cavs tightly. When a Cavs player finally took a shot, he missed. Golden State got the ball. Now the Warriors were in control.

FUN FACT

Durant was the Warriors' leading scorer in every game of the 2017 NBA Finals.

It was time to ice the game. The Warriors dribbled around. They passed. Then they passed again, this time to Durant. Cleveland fouled him with 12.9 seconds left. Once again, Durant was ready. He stepped to the **free-throw** line. He nailed the first one. Then he nailed the second. The Warriors now led by three. Cleveland would need a miracle to come back. Against Durant and the Warriors, that was not to be. Golden State went on to win 118–113.

Durant was new to the Warriors. But on the biggest stage, he shone. The Warriors won the series in five games. It was their second championship in three years. And Durant was named Finals Most Valuable Player (MVP).

Durant, right, celebrates the 2017 NBA title with teammates Klay Thompson, left, and Stephen Curry.

CAREER TIMELINE

1988

September 29, 1988
Kevin Durant is born in Washington, DC.

2006
Durant attends the University of Texas to play basketball for the Longhorns.

2006

2007

June 28, 2007
After one season at Texas, Durant enters the NBA Draft and is chosen second overall by the Seattle SuperSonics.

2008
Durant wins Rookie of the Year. After the season, the SuperSonics move to Oklahoma City, Oklahoma, and become the Thunder.

2008

2012
Durant leads the Thunder to the NBA Finals. He leads the team in scoring, but the Thunder lose to the Miami Heat.

2012

August 12, 2012
Durant wins an Olympic gold medal with the US men's basketball team.

2012

2014

2014
Durant wins the NBA MVP Award.

2016
Durant signs with the Golden State Warriors on July 7. On August 21 he wins his second Olympic gold medal.

2016

June 8, 2018
Durant wins his second NBA Finals MVP Award as the Warriors beat the Cleveland Cavaliers for the second year in a row.

2018

CHAPTER 2

DC Durant

They called it "The Hill." It was a steep part of L Street near Washington, DC. This was where young Kevin Durant got strong.

Kevin ran up the hill. Then he walked down backwards. Then he did it again. And again. Kevin had to keep track of how many times he did it. If he lost count, he had to start over. His basketball coach, Taras Brown, made him do this.

Kevin grew up not far from the Capitol in Washington, DC.

Brown knew it was tough. But it would make Kevin strong. Kevin's mom, Wanda, kept watch.

Kevin was born in DC on September 29, 1988. He and Wanda were very close. Kevin's father was not around when he was growing up. Wanda and her parents raised Kevin and his siblings.

It was tough on Kevin not having his father around. But he had his coaches as **mentors**. Brown and Charles "Chucky" Craig taught him about basketball and life. Craig encouraged Kevin to try out for basketball as a nine-year-old. Brown encouraged Kevin to take the game more seriously.

Hard work helped Kevin get to the top level of the sport.

Brown saw Kevin wasn't demanding the ball during games. He also thought Kevin didn't shoot enough. But Kevin knew he could do it. He said he wanted to rule the NBA.

"Then you got to listen to me," Brown said.

FUN FACT
Kevin dunked for the first time when he was in eighth grade.

Kevin was named co-MVP of the 2006 McDonald's All-American Game, a major high school showcase game. Both Kevin and co-MVP Chase Budinger later reached the NBA.

Kevin averaged 25.8 points and 11.1 rebounds during his lone season at Texas.

Kevin did. He practiced a lot. He worked on shooting. By high school, he was a top **prospect**. But he also suffered a big loss. In 2005, Craig was shot and killed. He was 35 years old. Kevin started wearing jersey No. 35 to honor him.

He wore that number at the University of Texas. He only played one season for the Longhorns. But it was spectacular. He was named national player of the year. After, Texas **retired** his No. 35. Kevin chose to enter the NBA Draft. He was chosen second by the Seattle SuperSonics. Kevin was done climbing the hill on L Street. But he had others to climb now.

The University of Texas

CHAPTER 3

The Real MVP

The camera lights came on. The room fell silent. Everyone wanted to hear from the 2014 NBA MVP, Kevin Durant.

His Oklahoma City Thunder teammates sat behind him. They had a playoff game that night. But first, Durant had some people to thank. He thanked teammate Russell Westbrook. He thanked the fans. Then he got to one last person.

Durant wipes away tears as he accepts his 2014 NBA MVP Award.

Wanda Durant

FUN FACT

The Lifetime TV network made a movie about Wanda Durant. It's called *The Real MVP: The Wanda Durant Story*.

"The odds were stacked against us," he said. "Everybody told us we weren't supposed to be here."

But this time Durant wasn't talking about a Thunder teammate. Durant was speaking about his mom, Wanda.

"You the real MVP," he concluded.

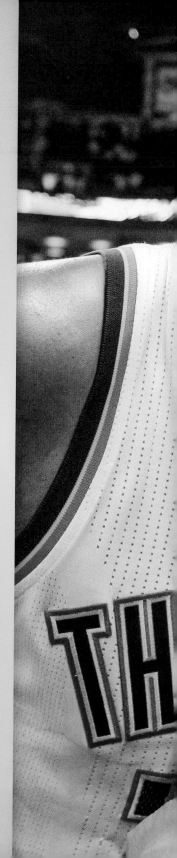

Wanda taught Durant many lessons. One of them was to give back. Durant thought back to his days as a kid. He had some challenges. But he had many people help him. He wanted to help kids succeed.

In February 2018, Durant donated $10 million to kids in his hometown. The money would help kids go to college. In June of that year, Durant heard about four special students. They were from DC. They were named Youth of the Year finalists by the Boys & Girls Club. Durant used to go there as a kid, too. The students reminded Durant of himself. He offered to pay for a year of college for each of them.

FUN FACT

Durant also has a company that invests money into new startup companies.

Wanda celebrates a 2014 playoff win with Durant.

Where Durant Has Been

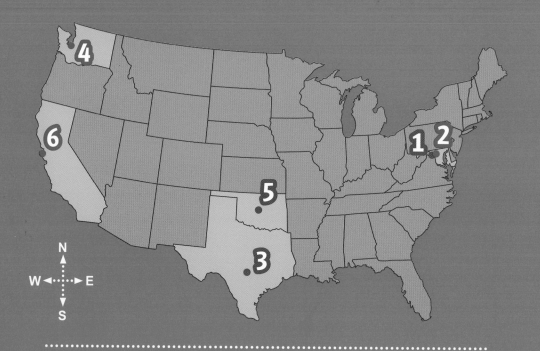

1 **Washington, DC:** Durant was born here.

2 **Prince George's County, Maryland:** Where Durant grew up.

3 **Austin, Texas:** Home of the University of Texas, where Durant played college basketball.

4 **Seattle, Washington:** Home of the former SuperSonics, who drafted Durant.

5 **Oklahoma City, Oklahoma:** The SuperSonics moved here and became the Thunder.

6 **Oakland, California:** Home of the Golden State Warriors, where Durant signed in 2016.

Durant likes connecting with people. He started up a YouTube channel in 2017. The channel lets fans see a different side of him. The channel got very popular. It had nearly 30 million views by 2019.

In 2018, Durant was leading the Warriors to another NBA title. He was all over the highlight reels. Fans wanted a piece of the action. Durant's jersey was the fourth-best seller in the NBA. Fans just wanted to be like Durant.

Durant plays basketball with a local team during a visit to China.

Warrior

Time was running out on Kevin Durant. His team needed him. It was his time to take over.

It was Game 7 of the Western Conference finals. Durant's Thunder were playing the Warriors. Oklahoma City was down 90–79. It was now or never.

Durant drained a three-pointer. Then he hit two free throws. After that, Golden State's Steph Curry turned the ball over. Durant went the other way. He drove to the hoop. But his path was blocked. So he pulled up for a jump shot. Swish! Just like that, the Thunder were only down four.

Oklahoma City

Durant passes under the hoop during Game 7 of the 2016 Western Conference finals.

But then it was Curry's turn. He scored the next three points. Then with time running out, Curry launched a three. He nailed it. That put the game out of reach. Durant was sad. It was hard to watch the Warriors celebrate. Durant wanted to do that someday.

In eight seasons, he had tried his hardest to win a title for the Thunder. It had not happened. He was ready for a new challenge. He was ready to win. Durant saw the Warriors' greatness up close. That was where he wanted to go.

Durant signed with Golden State on July 7, 2016. The next season, he led the Warriors to their second title in three years. He was MVP of the Finals. And Wanda was there to see it.

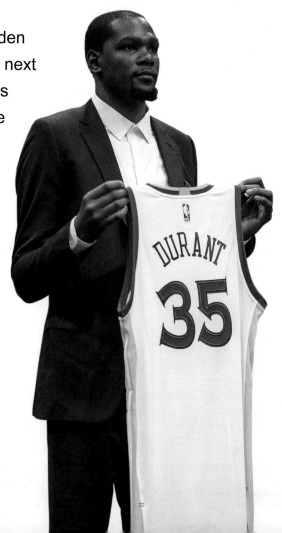

"We did it," he told her. "I told you when I was eight years old . . . we did it."

The Warriors offered Durant more than $25 million per season.

CAREER
STATS

Through the
2018–19 season

GAMES PLAYED	**849**
POINTS PER GAME	**27.0**
REBOUNDS PER GAME	**7.1**
SHOOTING PERCENTAGE	**.493**
THREE-POINT PERCENTAGE	**.381**

Winning one championship was not enough. Durant wanted another title. He and the Warriors made it back to the Finals in 2018. Durant was at his best in Game 3. He did not miss a shot until the second quarter. He scored 43 points total. He also added 13 rebounds. That helped keep the Warriors offense running. They won 110–102.

Durant averaged 29 points throughout the 2018 playoffs.

They dominated Game 4, too. The Warriors swept the Cavaliers. And Durant won another Finals MVP.

Growing up never stopped for Durant. He grew as a person and as a player. Now he was an MVP and a champion. But Durant was never satisfied. He had more to do.

GOLDEN SUMMERS

Durant has done a lot of winning with the Warriors. He has won even more playing for his country. Durant played in two Olympic Games with Team USA. The team won the gold medal each time. It never lost along the way. Durant was the leading scorer in both gold-medal games.

BEYOND
THE BOOK

After reading the book, it's time to think about what you learned.
Try the following exercises to jumpstart your ideas.

THINK

DIFFERENT SOURCES. Chapter One talks about the Warriors winning the 2017 NBA Finals. What resources are there that would have more information on these games? Where would you look to find them? What kinds of information would each source have that the others might not?

CREATE

SHARPEN YOUR RESEARCH SKILLS. The sidebar in Chapter Four discusses Durant's experience with the US Olympic Team. Where could you go in the library to learn more about the Olympic Games? What would you search for? Write up a plan for how you would start this research.

SHARE

SUM IT UP. Write a paragraph summarizing the key points of Durant's life as written in this book. Be sure to write this paragraph in your own words and do not simply copy the book's text. Share your writing with a classmate. What feedback does your classmate have?

GROW

DRAWING CONNECTIONS. Sports are often connected with other topics you might learn about in school. For example, sports use a lot of math and numbers. How is basketball connected to math? Create a diagram showing how these two topics are related. How does learning about math help you understand basketball?

RESEARCH NINJA

Visit *www.ninjaresearcher.com/0394* to learn how
to take your research skills and book report writing to the next level!

RESEARCH

DIGITAL LITERACY TOOLS

SEARCH LIKE A PRO
Learn about how to use search engines to find useful websites.

FACT OR FAKE?
Discover how you can tell a trusted website from an untrustworthy resource.

TEXT DETECTIVE
Explore how to zero in on the information you need most.

SHOW YOUR WORK
Research responsibly—learn how to cite sources.

WRITE

GET TO THE POINT
Learn how to express your main ideas.

PLAN OF ATTACK
Learn prewriting exercises and create an outline.

DOWNLOADABLE REPORT FORMS

Further Resources

BOOKS

Christopher, Matt. *On the Court with . . . Kevin Durant.* Little, Brown and Company, 2018.

Gitlin, Marty. *Kevin Durant: Basketball Star.* Focus Readers, 2017.

Nagelhout, Ryan. *Kevin Durant: Champion Basketball Star.* Enslow Publishing, 2018.

WEBSITES

FACTSURFER

Factsurfer.com gives you a safe, fun way to find more information.

1. Go to www.factsurfer.com.

2. Enter "Kevin Durant" into the search box and click 🔍.

3. Select your book cover to see a list of related websites.

Glossary

draft: Pro sports teams use a draft to choose new players to add to their rosters. Durant was chosen second in the 2007 draft.

free throw: Basketball players shoot a free throw when they are fouled. Durant hit a free throw to give the Warriors the lead.

invest: To invest is to lend money to something in order to help it grow. Durant invests in small companies.

mentors: Mentors are people who give advice to others to help them in their lives. Durant's basketball coaches were mentors for him as a kid.

prospect: A prospect is an athlete who has the potential to be very good. Durant was one of the nation's top prospects in high school.

rebound: A basketball player gets a rebound when he gets the ball after a missed shot. Durant brought down the rebound to start the next play.

retired: When a player's uniform number is retired, no other player can wear that number in the future. The University of Texas retired Durant's No. 35.

swish: A swish is when a basketball goes through the basket without touching the rim. When Durant shot the ball, it went right through the hoop. Swish!

Index

PHOTO CREDITS

The images in this book are reproduced through the courtesy of: Richard W. Rodriguez/AP Images, front cover (center); Rich Pedroncelli/AP Images, front cover (right), p. 3; Oleksii Sidorov/Shutterstock Images, front cover (background top); Torsak Thammachote/Shutterstock Images, front cover (background bottom); yhelfman/Shutterstock Images, p. 4; Tony Dejak/AP Images, pp. 5, 6–7; Marcio Jose Sanchez/AP Images, pp. 8, 23; Red Line Editorial, pp. 9 (timeline), 20, 25 (chart); icsnaps/Shutterstock Images, p. 9 (basketball); Orhan Cam/Shutterstock Images, pp. 10–11; Oleksiy Naumov/Shutterstock Images, p. 12; Kenneth Sponsler/Shutterstock Images, p. 13; LM Otero/AP Images, p. 14; f11photo/Shutterstock Images, p. 15; Sue Ogrocki/AP Images, pp. 16, 17; Eric Gay/AP Images, pp. 18–19; Alexander F. Yuan/AP Images, p. 21; Sean Pavone/Shutterstock Images, p. 22; Daniel Gluskoter/Icon Sportswire/AP Images, p. 24; Tony Avelar/AP Images, p. 25 (Kevin Durant); Ezra Shaw/AP Images, p. 26; Leonard Zhukovsky/Shutterstock Images, p. 27; niwat chaiyawoot/Shutterstock Images, p. 30.

ABOUT THE AUTHOR

Anthony K. Hewson is a freelance writer originally from San Diego, now living in the Bay Area with his wife and their two dogs.